BALINA

by Michael Sandler
illustrated by Michelle Shapiro

SCHOOL PUBLISHERS

Printed in China

ISBN 10: 0-15-351032-3
ISBN 13: 978-0-15-351032-8

Ordering Options
ISBN 10: 0-15-350602-4 (Grade 5 On-Level Collection)
ISBN 13: 978-0-15-350602-4 (Grade 5 On-Level Collection)
ISBN 10: 0-15-357957-9 (package of 5)
ISBN 13: 978-0-15-357957-8 (package of 5)

4 5 6 7 8 9 10   0940   12 11 10 09

During a summer day years ago, almost a hundred years ago to be exact, the people of Tampa Bay, Florida, were mighty surprised. A huge whale swam straight up to the shore.

Whales were rarely seen in the bay. In fact, they were never seen at all. As a result, people on shore were taken aback. The whale's actions were odd.

Then people were further surprised. The whale, now halfway out of the water, opened its mouth. Everyone stopped and stared. The whale sat there—half out of the water, half in—its mouth wide open. It didn't move at all.

One Tampa resident figured there must have been some reason for the whale's unfathomable behavior. The man walked across the beach. He wanted a closer look. It was a brave move.

Whale breath is awful. It smells of stinky fish and rotten seaweed. The man held his breath. He pinched his nose tightly shut. He moved forward. He stared inside the animal's mouth. "There is something in there," he thought. "Something is moving around inside."

He wasn't mistaken. A human being was on top of the whale's tongue. It was a child, a baby girl with striking blue hair, who was crawling around, very much alive. Braving the fierce smell, the man reached in. He grabbed the girl and pulled her out.

A crowd quickly gathered. They leaned over to inspect the child. Incredibly, despite arriving by whale, she was healthy. People wondered aloud, "Where did she come from? Did she fall off a ship? How could she possibly have survived?"

Try as they might, no one could come up with an answer. The whale, of course, wasn't talking. In any case, it left as soon as the girl had been taken from its mouth.

The girl was taken to a hospital where she was examined by doctors. Within a few days, she was adopted by a local family. The mystery of her aquatic arrival was never solved.

The family named the girl Balina. She thrived in their care and grew up healthy and strong. She grew so strong that her parents were amazed.

By the time she was about four—her parents had to guess her age—she could lift either of them off the ground. At about the age of six, while visiting a local farm, she lifted up a cow. The farmer's jaw dropped open in shock. When the poor animal started bellowing, Balina quickly set it down.

Balina was unusual in other ways as well. She rarely spoke. Instead, she made strange whale-like cries. She also had a strange love for water. Each day during the summer, Balina begged her parents to take her to the beach.

Her parents usually agreed. They would sit for hours, reading or playing cards, while Balina swam and swam. They had no fear for her safety. Without a single lesson, Balina could swim twice as well as any fish.

She never grew tired. Long swims into deep water were what she loved the most. Sometimes she would disappear for hours. Once she made it to Cuba and back before lunchtime. Another time, she was gone all day.

"Where did you go?" her mother asked when Balina finally returned.

"Around the world," Balina replied.

During the winter, Balina's parents didn't like going to the beach. It was too cold. It was too windy. This made Balina sad. She yearned for the water.

Instead of the ocean, she had to settle for the tub. Sometimes, she'd spend five or six hours bathing each day.

Of course, this created some problems. Her father was afraid that all the time Balina spent in the water would cause her to shrivel up and wither. Her brothers and sisters had a different concern. They could never get in the bath to get clean themselves. Finally, Balina's parents fixed the problem. They built a pool in the yard. She spent all afternoon there. The weather didn't matter. Balina went swimming rain or shine.

Balina went to school like other children. Despite her reluctance to talk, she did well in all her classes. She was nice. She was polite. She made plenty of friends.

Still, Balina was happier in the water than anyplace else. Because of this, she went to work in the harbor after graduating from high school—not doing what you might think, however. Balina started working as a tugboat.

That's right, she worked *as* a tugboat, not *on* one. Balina pulled ships in and out of the harbor herself. She was so strong that she could swim through the water towing a ship. To do so, she used a line fixed around her waist. No ship was too large. Even mighty cruise ships were no problem.

Locals grew used to watching her work. After a while, her escapades grew ordinary. Tourists, however, would always stop and stare.

"It's a girl, pulling a…boat!" they would shout.

"Yes, that's just Balina," came the tired response from the locals.

Real tugboat owners weren't pleased. They made lots of money. They charged big fees. Balina would do it for less. After all, she was really doing it for fun.

Her costs were few. She didn't pay any wages. She didn't pay for fuel. A nice big meal was all the fuel she needed. Her favorite food was a heaping bowl of baitfish and a plate of seaweed salad.

The tugboat operators were losing business. They weren't happy about it. One day, they got together and hatched a plan. They wrote to the mayor and complained about Balina. The mayor had once run a tugboat herself. She didn't want to betray her former buddies. Before Balina knew it, her work was gone. The mayor had passed a law. Only boats, not humans, could operate as tugboats.

Balina wasn't happy. Without her work, she felt like an outcast. Still, she took the change as best she could. She spent her free time exploring the world's oceans. She passed her days frolicking with dolphins and seals. Each evening, however, she always came back to Tampa. She never missed a family dinner.

One day, something happened that caused Balina to win back her job. A huge storm developed. It passed over the whole Gulf coast. Most ships tried to avoid it. Many made it safely back to harbor. One huge passenger vessel did not. It found itself caught in the storm.

The ship was driven into rocks not far from the coast. It was stuck, wedged in. Waves taller than Florida's tallest buildings pounded it. Soon, it would break apart.

From shore, the harbor masters watched helplessly. Staring through telescopes, they could see a rescue was needed, but no one could perform it. No ship dared challenge the storm.

Balina, however, was fearless. She jumped straight into the raging ocean. She swam right through waves that could tear a ship in half. In minutes, she had arrived at the stricken ship. She waved to the captain. Then, pushing off against the rocks, she freed the vessel from its trap.

The rocks had torn a gaping hole in the side of the ship. If she set it back down in the water, the ship would certainly sink. Balina flipped over on her back, still holding the ship up in the air. Then she kicked with her legs, all the way back to Tampa Bay with the ship safely above the water.

Balina hoisted the ship out of the water into a dry dock. There, passengers streamed off the ship. The captain ran up and hugged Balina. Soon, news of the rescue got around town. Balina's reputation grew and grew. Faced with pressure from the public, the mayor had no choice. She couldn't keep a hero out of a job. She cancelled the tugboat law, and Balina was free to work again.

Balina was cruising through the harbor again. She hummed her strange, whale-like song. She pulled ships into the pier. The tourists stopped and stared.

For years, that's how it went. Then one day, a group of whales appeared at the entrance to the harbor. They waited in the water, singing a melodic whale song. Balina looked at them and dropped her towrope. She turned to her mother and father who were sitting at a table on the pier. They looked up from their newspapers and saw the look in Balina's eyes. They knew they needed to let her go and explore the world with the whales. With that, they blew Balina a kiss as she swam off with the whales.

However, every year when the whales migrated, she returned home for dinner with her family and reported all her adventures.

Think Critically

1. What caused the whale's strange behavior at the beginning of the story?

2. What makes Balina unusual?

3. Would you like to have Balina's unusual characteristics? Why or why not?

4. How do you think the tugboat owners felt when Balina started working again?

5. How is this story similar to other tall tales you have read?

 **Social Studies**

Tugboat Tasks Look up *tugboat* in an encyclopedia. Read about the work a tugboat does. Then, share your findings with the class.

School-Home Connection Tell family members the story of Balina and why it is a tall tale. Then ask each person what extraordinary things they would like to be able to do if they were a character in a tall tale.